W9-BJM-921

THE SPACE MISSION ADVENTURE

Be sure to read all the
Clubhouse Mysteries!

The Buried Bones Mystery

Lost in the Tunnel of Time

Shadows of Caesar's Creek

SHARON M. DRAPER

#4

THE SPACE MISSION ADVENTURE

ILLUSTRATED BY JESSE JOSHUA WATSON

ALADDIN

NEW YORK   LONDON   TORONTO   SYDNEY   NEW DELHI

ALADDIN

An imprint of Simon & Schuster Children's Publishing Division
1230 Avenue of the Americas, New York, NY 10020
This Aladdin hardcover edition March 2012
Text Copyright © 2006 by Sharon M. Draper
Illustrations copyright © 2006 by Jesse Joshua Watson
Originally published as the series title *Ziggy and the Black Dinosaurs*.
All rights reserved, including the right of reproduction in whole or in part in any form.
ALADDIN is a trademark of Simon & Schuster, Inc., and related logo is
a registered trademark of Simon & Schuster, Inc.
Also available in an Aladdin paperback edition.
For information about special discounts for bulk purchases, please contact
Simon & Schuster Special Sales at 1-866-506-1949 or business@simonandschuster.com.
The Simon & Schuster Speakers Bureau can bring authors to your live event.
For more information or to book an event contact the Simon & Schuster Speakers Bureau
at 1-866-248-3049 or visit our website at www.simonspeakers.com.
Designed by Karina Granda
The text of this book was set in Minion.
Manufactured in the United States of America 0212 FFG
2 4 6 8 10 9 7 5 3 1
Library of Congress Control Number 2005037938
ISBN 978-1-4424-4225-2 (hc)
ISBN 978-1-4424-4226-9 (pbk)
ISBN 978-1-4424-4259-7 (eBook)

This book is dedicated to
all young people who dream
of reaching the stars.

1

ZIGGY LOOKED UP AT THE NIGHT SKY IN AMAZEMENT.
The weather had been clear and cold, and thousands of stars decorated the inky blackness of the night. "Awesome, mon," Ziggy whispered to his friend Rico, who stood shivering beside him. "They look like shiny pieces of hard candy floating up there, don't they?"

Rico stamped his feet and blew into his gloves. Even though he had on new, fur-lined boots and a down jacket, he felt chilled. "It's cold out here, Ziggy. Let's go look at the stars from inside your house."

Ziggy stretched both his bare hands up to the

sky. He wore no gloves, but he rarely took off his favorite hat, a fuzzy black, green, and yellow cap his mother had knit for him. "I feel like I could almost reach up there and pull a star out of the sky and bite it," Ziggy said with a laugh. "Let's go in, mon. You look like a chocolate Popsicle!"

The two friends hurried into the warmth of the house, where Ziggy's mom had mugs of hot chocolate waiting for them. "Thanks, Mrs. Colwin," Rico said as he sipped the warm drink. He was glad they weren't having a meeting of their club, the Black Dinosaurs, in their backyard clubhouse tonight. Ziggy, even though he had been born in the tropical climate of Jamaica, seemed to love the winter weather of Cincinnati, Ohio. He had wanted to meet as they had done all summer, but the chilly winter winds had chased the boys inside.

The doorbell rang, and Ziggy jumped up to answer it. "What's up, dudes?" Ziggy said in greeting to the other two members of the club, Rashawn and Jerome. "You want some hot chocolate?"

Rashawn, tall, thin, and always ready to go one-on-one at the basketball court, walked in wearing his favorite army boots and jacket. Jerome, shorter and stronger-looking, grinned at Ziggy, tossed off his leather jacket, and grabbed a mug of hot chocolate in each hand.

"It's really cold out there!" Jerome exclaimed as he sipped first from one mug, then the other.

"How you figure you get two cups of cocoa?" Rashawn asked.

"I'm tougher than the rest of you, so I need double the fuel!" he replied with a grin.

Rashawn took the last mug of chocolate, impressed that Ziggy's mom had known to make extra, and sipped it gratefully. "I just want to make sure I don't get the cup with the pickle in it!" He glanced at Ziggy, who, as usual, was stirring his chocolate with a thick green pickle.

"Why do you do that, man?" Rico asked, shaking his head.

"The pickle makes it taste better, mon. Besides, we were out of ketchup!" The other boys groaned, but they were used to Ziggy's strange food habits.

The four of them had been friends since first grade.

"Did you bring your Space Camp stuff?" Rashawn asked the other boys.

"It's right here in my backpack," Rico answered, pulling out a folder of forms and instructions.

"This is going to be so cool!" Jerome and Ziggy pulled out their paperwork as well. "I can't wait to get to Space Camp, mon," Ziggy exclaimed as he sucked the chocolate off the pickle. "Wouldn't

it be awesome to go into space for real?"

"Yeah," Jerome said. "I wonder what you have to do to be an astronaut."

"I never thought about it," Rashawn said. "But I suppose there's lots of training."

"You gotta learn how to read the instruments and fly the space shuttle," Rico offered. "And know what to do if you have to walk in space and fix something on the outside of the shuttle."

"I figure you need to practice what it feels like to be weightless so you don't throw up, mon!" Ziggy added.

"When we get to Space Camp, you practice that one by yourself—okay, Ziggy?" Jerome laughed, held his nose, and moved to a chair away from Ziggy.

"Let's go over this stuff, so the Black Dinosaurs Space Team is ready," Rico said. "I can't believe my dad is taking us all the way to Huntsville,

Alabama, for the weekend. I hope it's warmer there than it is here in Ohio!"

"Your dad is the bomb, mon," Ziggy exclaimed. "I know you only see him on vacations and stuff, but that is so cool that he's a pilot in the air force."

"Yeah, my dad really is all right," Rico replied. "He took me up in a jet last year on my birthday."

"Awesome!" Jerome said.

"Did you throw up?" Ziggy asked.

"Of course not! You focus on the strangest things, Ziggy." Rico shook his head.

"How long will it take to get there?" Rashawn asked.

"My dad says about seven hours by car. We go from Cincinnati, through Louisville, Kentucky, and Nashville, Tennessee, all the way down to Huntsville. But that's not counting stops at fast-food places or to see cool stuff," Rico told him.

"You think we can find our hometown chili dogs in Alabama?" Jerome asked. "Cincinnati makes the best chili in the world."

"You know, *every* city thinks its chili is the best," Rico replied with a grin.

"It's even better if you put jelly on your chili dogs, mon," Ziggy said cheerfully. "Gives them that extra-sweet flavor!"

"Yuck!" Jerome, Rashawn, and Rico all threw sofa pillows at Ziggy, who dodged them easily.

"So, what do we take with us besides bug spray?" Jerome asked as he glanced at the stacks of papers that Rico was handing each of them.

"There are no bugs in space, mon!" Ziggy said with authority, holding two of the sofa pillows on his lap.

"Yeah, but I bet there are plenty in Huntsville!" Jerome replied. "I take no chances, my man!"

"Let's see," Rico said, reading from the top page of the instructions. "Toothbrush and stuff, pajamas, socks, deodorant . . ."

"Don't forget that!" Rashawn said with a laugh.

"It also says not to bring portable music players or handheld video games," Rico continued.

"Not even my Mega Mighty Martian Blasters game?" Ziggy asked with dismay. "How will we practice dealing with invading Martian spacemen without that game?"

"Maybe we'll get real information instead of pretend video-game stuff," Rico replied sensibly.

"You mean it's not real? There aren't any Martians out there ready to attack Earth, mon?" Ziggy rolled off his chair and onto the floor, making zapping sounds like a space weapon.

"Probably not, Ziggy," Jerome told him. "But maybe you can ask somebody about it when we get there."

"If there's even just a possibility that Martian invaders might be real, I want to be ready, just in case. Martians are purple, have three heads, and spit fire, you know, unless they're in disguise. They can make themselves look like anything they want—a cat, a dog, even an Earthling."

"How do you know this?" Rashawn asked him.

Ziggy looked at him with surprise. "Because I've played the game a million times, mon!"

Rico laughed. "What else did you learn from that game, Ziggy?"

"Martians live in trees and eat rocks, mostly. But they have a special fondness for chocolate-covered pickles, just like I do, so they can't be all bad!"

"I bet the folks at Space Camp don't know any of this," Jerome told Ziggy.

"Well, I'll be sure to tell them! I guess the future of the planet is going to depend on me, mon," Ziggy said. "I can't wait to get to Space Camp!"

ONE WEEK LATER, ON A FROSTY, COOL MORNING, THE
four friends loaded their bags into the back of Rico's
dad's big SUV.

"It's so early, the birds aren't even up!" Jerome
said as he tossed his sleeping bag into the truck.

"I like the morning, mon! It's like the day smells
fresh and new—ready for adventures!" Ziggy twirled
around in Rico's driveway, excitement showing on
his face.

"I think that's your mom's sweet rolls you smell,
Ziggy," Rico told him. "Nothing better than hot cin-
namon rolls on a chilly morning."

"You're right. My mum was up hours ago making these for our trip. They're still warm."

"Are you gonna do something weird, like put ketchup on them or something?" Rashawn asked, wrinkling his nose as he climbed into the SUV with Jerome and Rico.

"Not my mum's sweet rolls, mon! Be sensible!" Ziggy climbed in the back row of seats with the others and gave everyone a roll even before they got to the end of the street. He made sure Rico's dad had two. "Must keep the driver happy, mon!"

Mr. Roman thanked Ziggy and drove smoothly down Interstate 75 for several hours. The boys dozed until he stopped at a gas station near Jellico, Tennessee.

"Would you look at that?" Rashawn said as he climbed out of the car and stretched.

"Wow!" Jerome echoed.

"That's the biggest dinosaur and Ferris wheel I've ever seen, mon!" Ziggy said with awe. "And look at that rocket ship!"

Mr. Roman chuckled. "I think they designed this

place so kids could stretch their legs and stretch the wallets of grown-ups as well."

"Now *that's* a dinosaur worthy of the Black Dinosaurs club," Rico said as they walked around the huge green model.

Mr. Roman snapped a photo of the boys as they mugged with the dinosaur.

"The dinosaur looks fake," Rashawn commented as the boys crammed close to see the result, "but we sure look good."

"I'm going to gas up the car. You guys look around a bit, and we'll leave after we eat," Mr. Roman said.

"That rocket looks pretty realistic," Jerome said. "Do you think it can really fly?"

"Naw, it's just a model like the dinosaur. I want to see the *real* stuff. I wonder what they'll have at Space Camp," Rico mused.

"Maybe that's where the Martian invaders will be hiding," Ziggy said as he patted the rocket ship. "Maybe disguised as dinosaurs like that one."

"You're always talking about Martians, Ziggy," Rashawn said with a sigh. "If you're so sure they

"Roadside Dinosaur"

exist, why haven't you ever seen one?"

"I don't know, mon! Maybe I have. I told you they use different disguises." Ziggy looked around, pretending to search for hidden aliens.

"Well, the Ferris wheel over there—maybe the one they flew in on—seems to be broken, so let's go inside and get something to eat. I'm starved," Rico said.

For four hours, the boys played a marathon state license plate bingo game, a noisy and confusing version of I Spy, and sang every camp song they'd ever learned. Finally, the boys looked excitedly out the window at their first glimpse of the U.S. Space and Rocket Center in Huntsville. Black and white rockets of various sizes stretched majestically into the sky as if waiting to be launched. Mr. Roman looked relieved as they pulled into the lot.

"Wow! And you thought that play rocket in Jellico was cool. Look at all those space vehicles!" Rashawn gaped with wonder. Standing several hundred feet tall, the largest rocket, painted with huge black and white rectangles, loomed boldly before them.

"Is that real, Dad?" Rico asked.

"Yes, son. That's the *Saturn Five*—the real thing. It was the largest operational launch vehicle ever produced. It's more than 363 feet high. If you could stand a football field on its end, the rocket would be taller. That's the kind of rocket that goes to the moon."

"To the moon," Ziggy repeated, his voice full of awe. "Wouldn't it be cool to walk on the moon you see up in the sky every night?"

The other boys nodded in agreement. "The rest of the rockets and rocket boosters and shuttle orbiters you see are real as well," Mr. Roman continued. "Some of them are models that were used for planning and practice, and some have actually flown in space."

"Hey, it's not cold here—must be at least seventy degrees," Jerome said as he took off his heavy jacket.

"Thanks for driving us, Mr. Roman," Rashawn said, helping him unload the bags. "I know we can be a pain in the butt sometimes."

Rico's father smiled. "I was a kid once, Rashawn. I'm glad the four of you are such good friends. I just wish we'd had something as cool as Space Camp when I was your age." He looked around at the towering rockets with almost as much awe as the boys.

Ziggy, for once, was speechless. He gazed at the

rockets and jets and space equipment that decorated what was called Rocket Park and just stared silently, a look of wonder on his face. "Awesome, mon," he whispered.

A Space Camp representative came to meet them as they headed to the registration area. A red, white, and blue sign read WELCOME TO U.S. SPACE CAMP AND U.S. SPACE AND ROCKET CENTER—THROUGH THESE DOORS ENTER AMERICA'S FUTURE ASTRO-NAUTS, SCIENTISTS, AND ENGINEERS.

"That's me, mon!" Ziggy said, swaggering a little. "Space soldier in training!"

"My name is Stanley," a young man in a navy blue Space Center T-shirt greeted them, shaking first each boy's hand, then Mr. Roman's. "Welcome to Space Camp!" He checked his list. "The four of you are here for Pathfinder Camp, right?"

"That means we get to do a mission, doesn't it?" Rashawn asked.

"Sure does," Stanley replied.

"A mission?" Ziggy asked. "What does that mean?"

"Your counselor, Samantha, will explain it all.

Every camper is assigned to a group that has a cool name—the four of you have been assigned to Team America."

"Awesome," Rico whispered.

"You gonna tell us how to prepare for a Martian invasion?" Ziggy asked.

Stanley laughed. "I bet you can get to the ninety-ninth level on Mega Mighty Martian Blasters, can't you?"

Ziggy's eyes grew wide. "How'd you know, mon?"

"I know my way around the galaxy," Stanley replied with a wink. "I'm not sure if we'll have time this weekend to get to Martians, but I guarantee you'll go home with more information about space than you ever dreamed of," he assured Ziggy. "Let's get you guys signed in."

They hurried through the registration process, getting name badges, bed linens, and Pathfinder T-shirts. "Who wants a top bunk?" Stanley asked as they headed toward the stairs to the sleeping quarters he called the Habitat.

"I do!" Rashawn said enthusiastically.

"Me too, mon!" Ziggy echoed him. "It's closer to outer space."

"Three feet up isn't going to make much difference, Ziggy," Jerome said. "I'll stay close to the ground. I may need to escape in a hurry."

"I'll take a bottom bunk too," Rico said. "Just seems safer."

"Okay, we have two up and two down. Let's get going," Stanley said.

The four boys grabbed their gear and the bed linens and T-shirts they'd been given and hurried up the stairs.

Rico said a brief good-bye to his father, who had decided to spend the weekend playing golf nearby. "I'll see you guys at graduation!" he called out to the boys, who were noisily climbing the stairs to the Habitat. They waved and didn't even notice when he left.

"It looks like an army barrack!" Rico said in dismay as they entered the room they'd been assigned to. There were a total of seven narrow beds, five of them top bunks. Underneath three of the top bunks were desks. The room was clean, bare of the carpet and wallpaper and room decorations the boys were used to at their homes, and very, very small.

"Most astronauts are in the military, you know," Stanley told them.

"That never occurred to me," Rico said thoughtfully.

"What about bugs?" Jerome asked. "Have you seen any insects crawling or flying around the Habitat? I like to be prepared, you understand."

Stanley chuckled. "Not that I'm aware of, Jerome. No more than the usual small bugs that you'd ordinarily find in Alabama this time of year. Certainly nothing dangerous. The dorms are cleaned and sanitized between each group of Space Campers, if that will make you feel any better."

"Thanks, man," Jerome said. He kneeled down on the concrete floor and peered under the bed, anyway.

Ziggy turned around in circles several times, searching the room with a quizzical look on his face.

"What are you doing, Ziggy?" Rashawn asked as he made up his bed.

"Something's missing, mon," Ziggy said.

"Well, it's not fancy, but it's got beds and lights and a place to store your gear," Stanley offered. "The bathroom's right outside, in this hall."

"That's not it, mon. *There's no television in this room!*" Ziggy stated, his arms stretched out dramatically.

Stanley laughed. "Of course not. You won't need it, you won't miss it, and you won't have time for it. By the time you get back to the Habitat tonight, you'll be exhausted and glad to see these lumpy bunks."

"Oh, I'll miss it, mon. I already do," Ziggy said with a sigh.

"Who will be in the other three bunks?" Rico asked.

"Three boys from Georgia," Stanley replied. "They're in the same grade as you guys."

Rashawn looked a little surprised. "Somehow I thought it would just be the four of us here. I never even thought about the other kids who'd be coming to Space Camp."

"Just a few rules," Stanley announced. "No eating

in the Habitat—we have a great cafeteria that will feed you well. No loud noises after lights-out. No girls in the boys' Habitat. No boys on the girls' floor. Just general common sense rules."

"Girls? You got girls here?" Rashawn asked with interest.

"Sure. The girls' Habitat is downstairs. Women can be astronauts too, you know," Stanley said. "We probably have as many girls here this weekend as boys. As a matter of fact, the rest of your team is probably the girls from the school in Georgia."

"Cool," Rico said. "This place is gonna be really cool."

3

SAMANTHA, THEIR COUNSELOR FOR THE PATHFINDER camp, had curly brown hair, a sprinkling of freckles on her nose, and a broad smile for her team as they met on the grass near the huge Pathfinder Shuttle that rested like a great beast on display. She wore the same navy blue shirt and beige pants that identified all the counselors, and she carried a clipboard that held a schedule for the day and the names of all the members of Team America.

Ziggy, Rico, Rashawn, and Jerome, dressed in their crisp, new, white Space Camp T-shirts, waited expectantly with the rest of their team as Samantha took attendance and made the effort to learn everyone's name.

"We're going to have a wonderful time here," she told the group with a smile. "We'll be up at dawn every morning, and back to the Habitat to rest at nine or ten each night."

"Long day, mon. When do we eat?" Ziggy asked.

"You'll get breakfast, lunch, and dinner," Samantha explained. "And I bet you'll like the food—it's pretty kid-friendly. Pizza, Tater Tots, fries, chicken fingers—stuff like that."

"Sweet!" one of the girls in the group said.

"You got chocolate-covered asparagus?" Ziggy asked with a grin.

"Ooh, yuck!" another girl said.

"What about hamburgers with jelly?"

Samantha laughed. "It's going to be easy to remember you, Ziggy. You have quite an imagination."

"He's serious, Samantha," Rashawn explained. "Ziggy has the strangest eating habits in the world!"

"Well, maybe tonight at dinner you can show

me how to dip my French fries into my chocolate pudding!" Samantha told Ziggy.

"I'm going to like her, mon! She understands me!" Ziggy put his hand to his heart and fell to the grass, kicking his legs in the air. The rest of the kids in the group cracked up.

The other three boys who shared bunk space with Ziggy and his friends were Neil, Alan, and Cubby, sixth graders from a small private school in Georgia. Neil and Alan were twins. With fiery red hair that stood up in little spikes, and tall, skinny frames, they were easy to spot from a distance, but a little hard to tell apart even up close. Cubby wore a baseball cap turned backward and what had to be size-twelve tennis shoes. He had already impressed the other boys with his knowledge of space history.

"That shuttle is the *Pathfinder*, you know," he said, pointing to the giant shuttle that was mounted fifty feet above their heads.

"How big is that sucker?" Jerome asked. "I feel like a bug standing under it."

"Well, the three parts you see are the orbiter—

that's the shuttle that carries the astronauts—and the external fuel tank—the thing that looks like a giant hot dog—and the solid rocket boosters. Those are the two white tubes. When they're full of fuel, they weigh over a million pounds each."

"Wow." Everyone in the group was silent, in awe of the giant space vehicle above them.

"Can it fly to the moon or to Mars, mon?" Ziggy asked.

"Well, this one doesn't fly at all, but shuttles aren't designed to fly so far away. For that, you need something like a *Saturn* rocket. Right, Samantha?" Cubby asked in a voice that said he knew she'd agree with him.

"Yes, Cubby, you're right. It looks like we have a space expert on our team."

Neil and Alan, the twins, rolled their eyes as if they'd heard Cubby's space facts many times before. "Did you know that these two were named for astronauts?" Cubby asked the rest of the team.

"How do you know, Cubby? You weren't there!" Alan said.

"But you told me, and your mom said it was true. I think it's really cool," Cubby said with a wistful look on his face. "I wish my mom had named *me* after a space hero."

"So who are you named after?" Rashawn asked Neil.

"I'm named after Neil Armstrong, the first man to walk on the moon," Neil explained.

"And Mom and Dad named me after Alan Shepard, first American man in space," Alan said. "Our parents are engineers and work for NASA—I guess they have high hopes for us."

"You're lucky, mon," Ziggy told the boys with a laugh. "She could have named one of you after Sally Ride, the first *woman* in space!"

Neil rolled his eyes. "Our three-year-old sister, of course, is named . . ."

"Sally!" Alan finished. Ziggy and the others laughed.

"I'm glad to know we've got a group who's really interested in space," Samantha commented. "I'm proud to have each of you on Team America." She then had each team member do a little introduction. The girls on their team, all students from Alan, Neil, and Cubby's school, were Amy, Jessica, and Nicolina.

Ziggy begged to introduce himself first, by jumping up and down and waving his arms wildly in the air. His braids bounced around his head as he moved. Samantha laughed and nodded at him to begin.

"I'm Ziggy, and I'm here to find out about Martians, mon!" Ziggy told the group. "I may want to be an astronaut one day, and I need to know what Martians look like when I get into space! And if they get here first, I want to be able to speak their language and say hello."

"There's no such thing as Martians or any other beings from other planets," Cubby said with authority.

"Have you ever been to Mars or Venus?" Nicolina asked Cubby. Her voice sounded whispery.

"Of course not!" Cubby answered.

"Then you don't really know for sure, do you?" Amy added with a smile.

"Is it possible there's anybody living on other planets, Samantha?" Rico asked.

"Well, anything is possible, Rico. That's why space exploration is so exciting! We're looking for answers to those and thousands of other questions. But I doubt if you'll find little green people like in comic books."

Ziggy made no comment, but he glanced up at the clear blue sky and grinned.

"Well, let's get started," Samantha told the group. "Our first tasks are a general orientation to space history and a movie in the Spacedome!"

"Ooh, are we gonna see *Space Creatures from the Ghost Galaxy*?" Rashawn asked. "It came out last week, and I heard it was really good."

"None of that science fiction stuff," Samantha replied. "What you're going to see is *real*! Real scientists in space. Weightlessness. Liftoffs with all the smoke and noise. What Earth really looks like from space. It will blow your mind."

"Cool!" the kids replied. They headed down the path to the Spacedome.

"When do we get to go on some of the rides?" Jessica asked Samantha as they walked.

"Oh, those aren't rides, Jessica. They're simulators, designed to show you what it feels like to walk, or move, or be propelled in space. We'll do quite a bit of that tomorrow," Samantha explained.

"I can't wait!" Jessica said.

The group passed a small, marble monument about four feet high. Piled on top of it was a large stack of bananas. "What's that, Samantha?" Rico asked.

Samantha stopped the group and said, "Gather around, kids. This is a good story. The very first beings in space weren't people, but animals. The first dog, sent up by the Russians, in 1957, was a little terrier named Laika. Unfortunately, she didn't survive the flight. She died in space."

"Oh, that's so sad," Jessica said softly.

"So, what's up with the bananas?" Rashawn asked. A few flies buzzed above the fruit.

"This monument is for Miss Abel and Miss Baker, the first monkeynauts!"

"Monkeynauts? That sounds like something I'd make up," Ziggy said.

"Yes, the first Americans in space were monkeys," Samantha explained. "They were launched into space and returned safely. Miss Baker lived to be twenty-seven years old—which is *really* old for a monkey! Visitors to the Space Center often leave bananas there in her honor."

"So what happens to the bananas?" Neil asked. "Do they just sit there and rot?"

Samantha looked at the group, a mischievous grin on her face. "No one knows for sure," she said mysteriously. "But every evening the bananas disappear, and new ones are placed there every day."

"Aliens, maybe?" Ziggy asked hopefully.

"I seriously doubt it, Ziggy!" Neil told him. "Spacemen aren't real."

As their team headed down to the Space Center Museum, Ziggy glanced up at a couple of squirrels chattering at each other in one of the many trees that lined the path.

"Hey, Rico," he whispered. "How do we know those squirrels aren't visitors from another planet?"

"Because they're squirrels, not Martians!"

"But how do you know for sure? It could be a really clever disguise," Ziggy insisted.

"Wouldn't this be the logical place to land and hide and observe humans? Nobody would even notice the ship they flew in if it looked like one of ours!"

"We've got enough real stuff to figure out here, Ziggy, without making up wild stories about alien squirrels." Rico opened the door to the Space Museum, where they would learn about early space travel. Jerome and Rashawn trailed behind, happily talking to the three girls from Georgia.

There were so many visitors touring the Space Center, the children paid very little attention to the attractive African-American lady in a navy blue Space Academy jumpsuit who was walking just ahead of them. She glanced back at them as they talked about aliens, looked as if she was about to say something, but then hurried on into the building without speaking. Samantha looked at the woman as if she recognized her, but the lady seemed to be in a hurry, so Samantha let the moment pass.

"So who eats the bananas every night?" Ziggy asked as they entered the hall full of displays of real space suits and actual lunar vehicles.

"It couldn't be the squirrels—they don't eat

fruit. They eat nuts and stuff like that."

"See what I mean?" Ziggy said with a laugh. "I read somewhere that Martians love bananas, mon. Maybe we've got a mystery here after all!"

THAT NIGHT, AFTER AN IMAX MOVIE IN THE
Spacedome that showed what it would be like to be
in space, several lectures on early space history, a
lengthy practice for their "mission," during which
they would pretend to be real members of a team
launching a rocket into space, and building their
own model rockets, the Pathfinder team dragged
themselves wearily to the Habitat.

Cubby and the twins headed for the showers
while Ziggy and his friends got ready for bed.

"Now I see why there's no television in here,"

Jerome said as he pulled off his T-shirt. "They really keep us going!"

"Didn't that shuttle look awesome in the moonlight?" Ziggy whispered dreamily. "It looked like it could just take off and head for the next galaxy."

"Yeah, it did look powerful," Rico agreed. "It's hard to believe it can't fly."

Ziggy looked thoughtful. "I still think it's a very clever disguise for visitors from another planet. Remember that story we read about in our mythology book about the Trojan horse?"

Jerome nodded. "Yeah, that was a cool story. The Greek soldiers put a giant wooden horse outside the gates of Troy, and the Trojans brought it into the city because they thought it was a gift."

"But the Greek soldiers were hiding inside, and when everyone was asleep, they crept out of the wooden horse and attacked the city," Rashawn said.

"No one suspected that big old horse had secret soldiers hiding inside, mon!" Ziggy said excitedly.

"Maybe there are space warriors hiding inside that shuttle."

"That shuttle has been sitting there for years, Ziggy. If bad guys from space are inside it, why haven't they come out and attacked yet?" Rico asked reasonably.

"I think they were waiting for us to get here, mon!" Ziggy said.

Jerome threw a pillow at Ziggy and laughed. "Well, I hope they don't come out of there tonight. I'm sleepy!"

"I wish I could climb up there and look inside it," Ziggy said quietly.

"First of all," Rashawn said as he sat in the middle of the floor taking off his socks, "you act like this is a science fiction movie. There are no secret creatures lurking inside that space shuttle." He threw his smelly socks at Ziggy, who ducked.

"Also," Jerome added, "I heard somewhere that they filled it up with cement when they mounted it there, to make sure space-happy kids like you don't try anything. There would be nothing to see even if you could somehow climb the one hundred feet to the top of it."

"Besides," Rico said, "if you so much as put your big toe outside the door of this Habitat tonight, alarms will ring, adults will show up in their nightclothes—a horrible thought—and you'll be sent home before the moonlight has time to shine on your face."

"You know what, Ziggy," Rashawn said. "You'd get us all in trouble and make our team look bad if you tried something like that."

"Yes, but we're the Black Dinosaurs club—shouldn't we be solving a mystery while we're here?" Ziggy asked.

"The only mystery I care about right now is what happened to my pj's!" Rico said as he dumped out his bag of clothes.

"You're sitting on them," Cubby told him with a laugh as he climbed into his bunk. Rico grabbed the pajamas and stuffed his other clothes back into his bag.

"Hey, don't worry. Ziggy is no fool, mon! But I can dream, can't I? This whole place is about learning the science to help make dreams come true. Maybe one day I can do that." He climbed into his top bunk. "But for now, I'm getting some sleep and dreaming of ways to get to space." He pulled the covers over his head.

The next morning, the boys woke to an early wake-up call and a breakfast of waffles and eggs. For their first activity, Team America headed over to the Multi-Axis Trainer, which Samantha called the MAT. A little nervous, each camper in the group shifted from one foot to the other as Samantha adjusted the straps and checked it for safety.

"It looks like a giant eggbeater," Ziggy said.

"Pretty big eggs," Rico said with awe in his voice.

"Martian eggs, of course, mon," Ziggy said, trying to sound unconcerned.

"It's designed to show you how your body would react if you were in a space vehicle that went into a tumble, so it goes upside down and around and around—almost at the same time," Cubby explained.

"You ever been on one?" Jerome asked.

Cubby shook his head. "I know a lot of this stuff because I've read about it in books, but I've never been on any of this equipment," he admitted.

"Who's going first?" Samantha asked.

Ziggy raised his hand. "Since I fully intend to be a real astronaut," he announced boldly, "I'm gonna be the first to see what it feels like to get your guts scrambled!"

He walked over to the circular-shaped machine, which was about eight feet tall and four feet wide. It was made of about thirty rounded metal bars that curved around the astronaut-trainee's seat. In the center of it a leather-cushioned chair with crisscross shoulder straps, arm and leg restraints, and a sturdy seat belt waited for Ziggy.

Samantha helped Ziggy climb into the seat, strapped him in carefully, and asked, "Are you ready, Ziggy?"

He nodded, and she stepped over to the controls to turn the machine on. "Keep your eyes open," she suggested. "That way, your body will know where it is and you won't get dizzy."

"I hope my body knows that," Ziggy told her quietly.

"His face looks just like it did the day he got called to the principal's office for letting that stray dog in school and hiding it all day," Rashawn whispered to Jerome.

"Do you think he'll throw up?" Rico asked.

"I hope not!" Cubby said. "That wouldn't be a pretty sight."

The MAT's motor began to hum, and then to turn. Faster and faster, up, down, around, upside down, and sideways. Over, under, through, and back again. Ziggy's braids flew wildly—like branches in a windstorm—but his body stayed safely glued to the chair. "Wheeee!" he cried out.

"How is it, Ziggy?" Alan asked from the benches where the rest of the kids waited their turn.

"Amazing, mon!" Ziggy managed to say as he was whipped around and around.

Finally the machine stopped, and the MAT chair returned to its upright position, swaying just slightly as Ziggy waved at his friends. He jumped down

triumphantly and sauntered over to the bench as Jessica ran forward to take her turn.

"Did you feel like you were going to throw up?" Rico wanted to know.

"No, mon. I didn't even get dizzy. It was the most fantastic thing I've ever done!"

"What was it like while you were spinning?" Cubby asked. "Real astronauts train on equipment like this, you know."

"It was like the floor and the ceiling and the walls were moving, not me. They bounced around in front of me faster than I could even think about it. My body always felt like it was two seconds behind what I was seeing and feeling," Ziggy explained.

"Cool!" Jerome said. "Hey Samantha, can I be next?"

All of the team members got turns on the trainer, grinning with satisfaction when they finished.

Ziggy asked immediately, "What's next, Samantha?"

"We're going to the One-sixth Gravity Chair trainer—the one that lets you see what it feels like to walk on the moon," she replied.

"Now *that's* what I'm talking about!" Ziggy said eagerly.

"What does it feel like when you're on the moon, Samantha?" Jessica asked. She twirled her hair between her fingers.

Samantha laughed. "Well, the last time I was there, it was snowing!"

"Huh?" Jessica looked confused.

"She's just teasing you, Jessica," Cubby said. "Only twelve astronauts have actually walked on the moon for real."

Samantha touched Jessica on the shoulder. "I'm sorry. I shouldn't have made light of your question. Cubby's right. Very few people have walked on the moon. But we do know that the moon's gravity is one-sixth of the earth's."

"That means that if you weigh sixty pounds on earth, you only weigh ten pounds on the moon. Right?" Rico asked.

"Absolutely!" Samantha replied.

"And if you can jump five inches off the ground here on Earth, you should be able to jump thirty inches high on the moon," Cubby added.

"You could jump *over* the basket on the moon," Jerome said dreamily.

"I could make baskets and dunk for days!" Rashawn said, pretending to make a jump shot. "NBA coaches would all want me on their team!"

"Yeah, but all your games would have to be on the moon!" Cubby said with a laugh.

"It's all good, mon!" Ziggy said as he tried to jump as high as he could on the sidewalk. Jerome, Rico, and Rashawn jumped with him, and the twins and Cubby joined in as well. Leaping and laughing, they headed toward the building where the 1/6th Chair sat waiting for them.

The ground beneath the chair was uneven and had been designed to look like the surface of the moon, with craters and hills. The chair, suspended above this "moonscape," waited.

"It looks like a giant baby's jumper toy—you know, those things on springs they use to exercise little kids," Rashawn said.

This time, Rico was the first to try the equipment. Samantha strapped him in and then showed him how to walk, bounce, and jump with what felt like very little gravity. He grinned, leaped, and stretched his arms wide while the others cheered. "I feel like I can fly!" Rico said. "This is glorious."

"This skill will come in handy when I explore the moon and send my report back for cable news," Ziggy told the others as he was strapped in next and began to jump.

"Or maybe when you try out for the ballet!" Jerome called out. "You look like a dancer."

Ziggy just grinned and used his toes to push himself even higher and take larger leaps that helped him soar. He swayed his arms gracefully. "I should have been born on the moon!" he cried out. "This is *too* cool!"

"There are no hamburgers on the moon, Ziggy," Neil called out.

"Or pizza with pickles!" Rashawn added.

"I don't care, mon! I was born to fly!" Ziggy bounced to the side, leaped forward and back, reached toward the ceiling, and jumped higher than his own height. He was a picture of movement—arms, legs, hair—gracefully flowing across the room. He sidestepped and swayed and swerved, almost twirling with delight.

Ziggy didn't want his turn to be over. But Samantha reminded him that everyone deserved equal time, so Ziggy reluctantly let himself be unstrapped and returned to the world of normal gravity. He knelt down to retie his tennis shoes, which had come unlaced in all the jumping. Lying on the edge of the artificial moon surface, caught between the moonscape and the wooden floor, was a small, oddly shaped, shiny object.

"What's this?" he whispered. He reached over, grabbed the item quickly, and stuffed it into his pocket.

When he got back to the benches where the others were waiting their turn, he took a seat in the back. He took the glossy, stonelike thing he had found out of his pocket and examined it carefully. It was a dark, shimmery green color—like the color of grass after a rainstorm—totally smooth on one side, and rough to the touch on the back. It was about the size of Ziggy's thumb. He rolled it around in his hands, a slight frown on his face.

"What's that you got, Ziggy?" Rico asked as he walked back to where Ziggy was sitting. "Can I see it?"

Ziggy handed it to him. "I think it's not from this world," Ziggy said with a serious expression that was unusual for him.

"What makes you say that?" Rico asked as he peered closely at the object.

"It looks hard, but it feels a little soft. It looks like it would be cold to the touch, but it feels warm. I think it's something left by a space traveler." Ziggy spoke as if he meant it. For once, he wasn't laughing.

Rico didn't make fun of Ziggy's observation. Instead, he said, "Let's approach this scientifically, Ziggy. Let's talk about all the things it could possibly be before we decide it's from outer space."

Ziggy nodded, but he didn't seem convinced. "It looks like the back of one of those insects you find in the summertime—all shiny and metallic-looking," he said.

"Are you sure it's not just a piece of dead bug?" Rico asked thoughtfully.

"What's that you said about bugs?" Jerome asked as he joined them. "I got bug spray in my backpack, you know, just in case."

"You won't need spray for this, mon," Ziggy said, "unless this is a space creature that can come back to life."

"What are you talking about?" Rashawn asked as he joined them. The other members of the team were taking their turn on the chair.

"Ziggy thinks he found a space artifact," Rico explained. The four of them took the object and examined it.

"Is it a piece of some kind of plant?" Rashawn asked as he sniffed it.

"It's too hard, I think," Ziggy said.

"Could it be broken off one of the pieces of equipment in this room?" Jerome offered. "They've got all kinds of space simulators in here. Maybe this is part of one of them."

"Maybe, mon," Ziggy said. "But I got a feeling that

this shiny green thing has some special meaning."

Rico looked at the object closely, then tapped it on the bench to listen to the sound it made. "I think it's made of metal, but I can't really tell. It's not rock, either—at least I don't think it is. Where did you find it, Ziggy?"

"I found it by the moonwalk simulator, and I think it came from outer space," Ziggy stated.

Rico, Jerome, and Rashawn shook their heads in disbelief. Team America had finished the simulation, and Samantha called them all to head for lunch.

"All we have to do is figure out why it's here." Ziggy carefully put the oddly shaped green thing back into his pocket.

AFTER LUNCH AND JUST BEFORE THEIR MISSION,
Samantha took Team America outside for a little
fresh air and to prep them for their pretend journey
into space. "Are there any questions?" she asked.

"We saw what it was like to walk on the moon,"
Rico said, "but what does it feel like to be weightless?
Does it feel like you're floating?"

"Well, I've never been lucky enough to actually
fly in space," Samantha replied, "but the astronauts
I've spoken to tell me that sometimes weightlessness
makes them throw up, and that it's hard to adjust to
being able to lift heavy objects with no effort."

"Can you sneeze in space?" Rashawn wanted to know.

"I'm sure you can," Samantha answered. "But I bet you can't guess what happens to the liquid that would come out of your nose." She grinned at the group.

"Tell us!" they demanded eagerly. Nicolina, a petite girl with a quiet smile, put her hand over her ears, pretending she didn't want to hear.

"Everything liquid in space, from water to fruit juice to mucus—even urine . . . ," Samantha began.

"Yucko, mon!" Ziggy said, making a face.

". . . forms into perfectly round balls. All the molecules are pulling on one another, so you see, with no gravity, a force we call surface tension makes the liquids ball up."

"Hey, since you brought it up, I gotta know this," Ziggy said slowly. "How do astronauts go to the bathroom, mon?"

"I wondered the same thing," Jerome admitted, "but I didn't want to ask."

"Even I don't know the answer to that one," Cubby said.

Samantha smiled as she looked at the group. "First of all, there are no flush toilets, so the toilets function with air instead. Basically, astronauts use the bathroom in something very much like a vacuum cleaner. Some of the shuttle crew call it Mr. Thirsty!" She laughed as the team members giggled with disgust and delight.

"This might be more than I can handle, mon." Ziggy covered his face with his hands, pretending to be upset. "Maybe I can't be an astronaut after all."

"A hose with vacuum suction is attached to the body, and urine is sucked through the hose. It's quite simple," Samantha explained, "and nothing to be embarrassed about. It's a normal human bodily function."

"What about women astronauts?" Jessica asked shyly. She blushed.

"There is an adapter for females," Samantha replied matter-of-factly. "And as long as we're on the subject, solid waste is also eliminated by means of suction devices. The opening is only about four inches in diameter, so an astronaut's *aim* becomes really important. They even have a practice device at the training center! It has a TV camera mounted in the toilet bowl so astronauts can learn exactly where to position themselves so everything comes out where it should!"

"Does that one have a name too?" Amy asked.

"For sure! It's called Target!" Samantha looked like she was having fun. "The astronauts have target practice before a mission."

"I thought target practice meant shooting at space invaders like on my Mega Mighty Martian Blasters video game, mon!" Ziggy said.

"Not this time, Ziggy," Samantha replied with a laugh.

"Oh, man!" Jerome said. "Big yuck!"

"So if an astronaut cut herself while in space," Nicolina asked quietly, "would the blood float like little balls as it leaves the cut?"

"Exactly!" Samantha said. "Little floating globules of blood."

"That's amazing," Nicolina replied, her eyes large with wonder.

Ignoring the boys who were making faces, Amy asked, "So if all liquid turns into little balls, how do they drink anything?"

"Good question, Amy," Samantha said. "You're right—they couldn't drink from a cup. They use straws, instead, used in specially designed containers that help them suck the liquid into their mouth."

"What do astronauts eat, mon?" Ziggy asked. "I'm almost afraid to know the answer after the last one you gave us."

Samantha laughed. "This time I think you can handle the answer, Ziggy. They eat MRE's, which stands for 'meals ready to eat.' Often they are dehydrated, which means water has to be added before they can be eaten, but sometimes it's stuff like candy or peanut butter or cans of pudding like you'd eat at home."

"Not like stuff I eat at home!" Ziggy told them with a laugh. "I bet the astronauts never had corn-flakes with gravy, or peanuts with prune juice, mon."

"Yuck!" Nicolina and Jessica said together.

"Where do astronauts sleep?" Rashawn asked.

"There are no beds, but they use something called sleep restraints to hold themselves in one place so they won't float around and bump into one another. When they're asleep, unless they're secured, their arms float straight up in front of their bodies. Their hair, too. I'm told it's a slightly spooky sight."

Ziggy looked thoughtful. "Samantha, have any space shuttles ever encountered any aliens, mon?" Ziggy asked. "I'm not being silly—I really want to know."

"No, Ziggy," she replied with the same serious-ness. "But I suppose there is always a first time. Now, let's get busy. It's time for our mission. Team America, let's launch!"

They marched over to Mission Control, where a group of specialists took over the training of the various Space Camp teams. Stanley was one of them. He carried a clipboard with the name and assign-ment of each member of Team America.

"First, each of you will be assigned a position,"

Stanley began. "If this were a real space shuttle about to be launched, what jobs do you think would be needed?"

"Captain of the astronauts!" Ziggy called out.

"Excellent!" Stanley said. "We call him the commander, and he or she is responsible for all crew activities inside the shuttle. We also need a pilot—someone to be in charge of flying the shuttle. Ziggy, you'll be the commander, and Cubby, you are the pilot."

"Awesome!" Cubby and Ziggy answered together.

"You know, with all my experience with the Mega Mighty Martian Blasters game, I should be really good at this," Cubby said.

"You have that game too, mon?" Ziggy asked Cubby enthusiastically.

"Sure," Cubby said. "I can get to the very top level!"

Ziggy looked at him with awe.

"We also need mission specialists," Stanley continued. "These are the folks who do space walks—we call them EVAs, or extravehicular activities—and payload specialists, the folks who work on the cargo or the experiments."

"Can I be those too, mon?" Ziggy asked.

"This is a team effort, Ziggy." Stanley checked his clipboard. "Jerome and Rashawn are the payload specialists, and Nicolina and Neil are the mission specialists."

"None of the experiments involves bugs in space, do they?" Jerome asked. "I saw a movie once about a bug that went into space and it came back and ate up a couple of cities! I don't think I've got enough bug spray for an attack like that!"

"You gotta understand, Stanley. Jerome gets really buggy when it comes to insects!" Rashawn explained as he made buzzing noises near Jerome's ear.

Stanley laughed. "I promise. No bugs."

"Don't you need somebody to be in charge of the computers on the ground?" Amy asked.

"Good, Amy," Stanley said. "The shuttle can't go up unless there is somebody on the ground making sure everything is safe. That person is called the flight director. He or she is in charge of the entire mission from ignition to touchdown. That will be your position, Amy." She grinned with delight.

"What about me?" Rico asked.

"Rico, you'll be the CAPCOM. That's the communications captain. You're in charge of all messages from ground control to the flight crew. Alan, you are the EVA officer. You are responsible for all the equipment that the shuttle crew is operating in space."

"Like when they do space walks and stuff?"

"Yes, your job is to keep them safe. It's scary out there—floating in space, connected to the shuttle by only a thin cord."

"Cool!" Alan said.

"Nicolina and Jessica—you two are assigned to the space station and will do various experiments that must be recorded and analyzed and sent back to Mission Control. You also get to wear the space gear and helmets and do the space walks!" Nicolina put her hand to her head and giggled. The two girls gave each other high fives.

"I want to wear a space suit and walk in space too, mon," Ziggy complained.

"Your job is critical to this mission, Ziggy," Stanley told him firmly. "Regardless of your position, a successful mission depends on the entire flight crew's coordination and skill. Are you with me, Team America?"

"Yes, sir!" they all replied enthusiastically.

"Then let's get this mission underway! We have just one hour to prepare for the launch in Mission Control, blast into space, go into orbit, do our experiments, and land safely."

"That's an awful lot to do in an hour," Rico commented.

"In real life it takes months, even years, to prepare a crew for launch and bring them back home. This is just to give you a taste of a real space mission."

"Since this is just a simulation—a pretend version of what real astronauts do—why can't we pretend we find space creatures?" Ziggy asked.

"Sorry, Ziggy. You'll have to do that when you get back home."

Team America marched into the area where the mission would take place, each one of them getting prepared in the various modules set up to be similar to what the inside of a real space shuttle or launch-pad would look like. All the team members got written scripts, headphones so they could communicate,

and even space suits so they really felt like they were doing their jobs.

Ziggy had a wonderful time pretending to be the captain of the shuttle on the mission of Team America, which they completed with great success. Their ship launched and landed safely, and they all felt proud.

But Ziggy kept thinking that something was missing. He fingered the strange object he had found and wondered if it would lead to the answers he wanted.

6

NOW THAT THE MISSION WAS OVER, IT WAS TIME to launch the rockets they had made the night before. Made of plastic, cardboard, and wood, and loaded with a real explosive device, the rockets had been carefully put together and decorated by each team member. Ziggy had painted creatures he called Martians all over his model, while Rashawn had painted a flag of the United States on his.

Team America walked leisurely along on the path that led to Area 51—the grassy knoll where rockets could be safely launched. It took about ten minutes to get there. Samantha, proud of her group for doing so well on their mission, let them laugh and joke as they hiked together, feeling not so much like strangers anymore but like a real team.

Cubby, still spouting facts about space travel, told them, "Did you know that a space shuttle goes 17,300 miles per hour? If we had really launched during our mission, we would have been going five miles per second!"

"Man, that's fast!" Rashawn said. "We coulda got here to Alabama from Ohio in just a few minutes."

The path was covered with leaves and dirt, and packed down where the sneakers of hundreds of other kids had walked, kids who had also been carrying rockets and maybe some dreams as well.

"The sky is so blue today, it looks like you could slice a piece of it and eat it like candy, mon," Ziggy said as he glanced up. He stopped for a moment, making Rico almost bump into him.

"Yeah," Jerome said, agreeing with him and pausing to look up at the sky as well. "And the clouds look like whipped cream."

"Are you guys gonna eat dinner or launch a

rocket?" Neil asked as he stopped and looked up also. "What's the big deal? It's just sky and clouds."

"No," Alan said, as he too stopped to look at the crystal-clear sky. "It's more than that. It's the place where the real rockets go."

Everyone was quiet for a moment, then Nicolina said softly, "I wonder what it looks like from the other side of the clouds. What I mean is, what do the astronauts see when they look down at the clouds from space?"

Samantha started to answer, but Cubby said, "Remember the movie we saw last night? From space the world looks like a giant ball, resting on nothing, just spinning in darkness and light—depending on where the sun is."

"Do you think astronauts can see the lines that divide countries?" Nicolina wanted to know. "I mean, like the line that separates the United States and Canada or Mexico. We see it on maps, but can they see it from up there?"

"Those lines don't exist," Samantha told them all. "Those are made by people who have divided the world into countries. In space, all that divides the world are mountains or rivers or deserts or oceans."

"That's deep," Rashawn commented.

"Can astronauts see clouds like we can?" Amy asked.

"Much more than clouds, I imagine. They see whole weather patterns—rainstorms and wind movement and such," Samantha explained. "Sometimes they see hurricanes forming in the ocean and heading toward land."

"That's really awesome, mon!" Ziggy said with feeling. The group quietly continued their walk to Area 51, glancing upward occasionally, but no one else spoke until they reached the place where the model rockets were to be launched.

When they got there, a series of launching pins had been set up and each person on the team got to set his or her rocket on the device that would send it soaring into the air. Two guides waited for them—a balding man with the navy blue shirt and khaki pants that all the counselors wore, and a woman with black curly hair who was chatting with him.

Samantha looked startled but said nothing. It was the same woman who had passed them on the sidewalk as they discussed the first monkeys in space.

"I bet my rocket goes all the way up to the moon!" Rico boasted.

"No way, mon! My rocket will surely go higher than yours because it's got Ziggy power! It's going to Mars for sure!"

"Actually," Cubby said, "these little rockets will only go a few hundred feet up in the air. You need liquid oxygen and solid rocket boosters to go into space."

"We know that," Rico said with a sigh. "It's just fun to dream."

The rocket launch captain told the group how to load the rockets onto the pins and showed them where to stand behind a glass partition when the rockets took off. The woman observed, but made no comment.

Ziggy's was the first to shoot off. "To Mars!" he shouted.

"*Kerpow! Ziiiiph!*" The rocket's tiny engine exploded, then the slender barrel of it whizzed into the air, over the trees, and then arched and landed on the grass several hundred feet away.

"Zowie!" Ziggy cried with excitement. "That was TOO cool!" He jumped up and down behind the observation partition. The woman gave him a genuine smile.

The rest of the team, one at a time, got to take a turn at shooting their rockets and watching them whoosh into the sky. Rashawn's rocket landed up in a tree. Jerome's exploded on the stand and never took off at all. Rico's rocket shot a little ways up, then seemed to change its mind and it fizzled on the grass. Nicolina's rocket seemed to go the highest and soar the longest. She smiled with great satisfaction.

"Good job," the woman who had been observing them said to her. "Your rocket was well-built, which was why it flew so well. You'll make a fine engineer one day."

"Me?" Nicolina said in disbelief.

"I was a little girl with dreams of building great

machines that would change the world one day," the woman told her.

"Did you?" Nicolina asked.

"I haven't changed the world yet, but I'm doing my best to make a difference!" she replied. "Don't be afraid to aim for the stars."

Nicolina smiled shyly and looked up at the bright sky.

AS THEY HEADED BACK DOWN THE PATH TO THE cafeteria for lunch, the woman who had watched their launches and spoken to Nicolina walked with them. Samantha chatted with her quietly, then stopped the group.

"Hey, Team America, I want you to meet somebody," she said. "This is someone you'll be really excited to know."

The attractive lady with the large smile grinned even wider. Her skin was the color of copper, and her softly curled hair rippled in the breeze as the wind whipped up a bit. She was tall and lean.

"She looks tough," Jerome whispered to Ziggy. "Like she could beat up a bad guy if she had to."

"You've been watching too many movies, mon!" Ziggy whispered back. "She's too pretty to be mean."

Samantha was grinning like she had found a puppy. "Team America—I want to introduce you to Denise Washington. She's a NASA astronaut."

"I'm really pleased to meet you, ma'am," Jerome said, using his best manners. He even reached out to shake her hand. She took his hand in her own and shook it firmly.

"Delighted," she said. Her voice sounded strong and confident.

"You've been in space?" Rico asked, awe in his voice.

"Not yet, but I'm on my way!" she replied.

"I read about you on the NASA website!" Cubby said excitedly. "You've been assigned to go on one of the next shuttle flights!"

"That's right, son. I'm assigned to *STS-116*, scheduled for next year sometime." She seemed impressed that he knew.

"Are you going to Mars, maybe?" Ziggy asked. He was breathing hard and almost dancing with excitement.

"No, not to Mars on this trip, but I hope to get as far as the space station."

"We just finished our Space Camp mission," Rashawn told her. "I was a mission specialist, in charge of payload."

She placed her hand on her jaw. "That's my job as well. I take care of the robotics."

"They got robots on the shuttles, mon?" Ziggy whispered to Cubby.

"Not like the robots on space movies that you're thinking about, Ziggy," Cubby whispered back. "The astronauts use robotic equipment to reach things and go places that humans can't safely go."

Ziggy nodded in understanding.

"Can you tell them a little about your training, Ms. Washington?" Samantha asked.

"Well, I've been in training to be an astronaut since 1999, but I'd worked for NASA for almost ten years before that. I guess I've done about every job there is. I've been a CAPCOM—"

"That was me!" Rico interrupted. "Communications was my job on our mission."

She smiled at him. "Great! I've also run tests on payloads, worked on simulations to make sure the real deal would work in space, and done vehicle testing and troubleshooting."

"Have you ever seen a shuttle be launched?" Neil asked.

"I have actively taken part in over fifty launches," she replied quietly.

"Wow." The voices of all the kids were filled with awe.

"What's it like," Nicolina asked, "when the shuttle blasts off?"

"It's the most exciting thing I've ever seen. The sky has to be clear blue—like today. The orbiter sits on the launchpad, its nose pointing to the sky, the two white solid rocket boosters sitting next to it, both of which are connected to the huge orange external fuel tank, waiting to take it to the heavens."

"Just like the one in Rocket Park, the one that you thought aliens were hiding in, Ziggy," Jerome said, teasing him.

"Yes," Ms. Washington continued. "Just like that one. And I'm sure there are no aliens hiding there." She chuckled. "In the control center, just like on the mission you guys simulated, the countdown begins. T-minus thirty minutes, then twenty, then ten."

Ziggy wriggled with anticipation.

"If everything is a go, the launch sequence continues to T-minus one minute. There's a buzz of activity, and everyone is tense, but we all know our jobs, so it's like controlled excitement. Each person has a specific and extremely important job, and critical decisions are made every single second."

"Like the flight director," Amy said. "That was what I did. It was a lot of responsibility, and our mission wasn't even real."

"You're right," Ms. Washington replied. "The pressure is enormous. Finally, the launch sequence counts down to the final seconds. Ten, nine, eight, seven, six, five, four, three, two, one. . . ." She paused.

"Don't stop!" they all cried out.

Ms. Washington smiled. "Even at this point, the launch could be aborted. But if everything is a go, you hear the words 'We have liftoff,' and the shuttle rises from the ground. It's the most amazing sight in the world."

"What does it look like?" Alan asked.

"Thick, heavy plumes of white smoke as the fuel is burned. A sound louder than the voices of a million football fans screaming at the same time. And a vehicle soaring into the sky, getting smaller every second. Nothing, and I mean nothing, is more awesome." She took a deep breath and looked at the sky as if she was remembering.

"What do you think it's like when you're *inside* the shuttle and it lifts off?" Rico asked.

"You know, I really can't wait to find out. We do years of practice at the Johnson Space Center in Texas. We have simulators that look and act and feel exactly like the real thing. They're a little like what you did today, except on ours, all the buttons and dials work and connect to real data equipment. Any mistakes we make could be disastrous, so we practice over and over again until we get it right."

"Can I be an astronaut one day?" Ziggy asked.

"Of course!"

"What do you have to do to qualify?" Jessica asked.

"First, you need a college degree in math or science or engineering—the more education the better," she began.

"Do you have to be in the army or navy?" Neil wanted to know.

"Not necessarily. Many of the astronauts are, but I'm not."

"Do you think it will help that I've been to Space Camp?" Cubby asked.

Ms. Washington laughed. "I'm sure it couldn't hurt."

"What about a physical? I guess you gotta be healthy," Rico said.

"Absolutely! The physical and mental tests are pretty tough."

"I know that women can be assigned to flights, but are you the only African-American astronaut?" Rashawn asked shyly.

"I'm glad you asked that question," Ms.

Washington answered. "Let me tell you just a little about minorities in our program. Since the program began, there have been more than a dozen African-American astronauts."

Jerome raised his hand. "I did a report on them for school, so I know that Robert Lawrence was the very first black astronaut, but he died before he could go into space," he explained. "Guion Bluford was the first African American to fly in space, and Ronald McNair died during the *Challenger* accident in 1986."

Ms. Washington looked pleased. "Excellent!" she said. "Do you know who was the first African-American woman in space?"

"You?" Ziggy asked hopefully.

"No, man!" Rico said. "She already told us she hasn't been up in space yet. It was Mae Jemison, wasn't it, Ms. Washington?"

"Yes! I am truly impressed by all your knowledge!" she said, pleasure in her voice. "We have also had six Hispanic astronauts."

"I knew that," Cubby said excitedly.

"You guys don't need me at all," Ms. Washington told the group. "I'd hire you to go in space tomorrow. You just need to be a little taller!" She laughed.

"Are there any other women astronauts?" Nicolina asked.

Ms. Washington nodded. "There's a Hispanic woman, Ellen Ochoa, in the program now," she told the group. "She's been on four space flights. There are some Hispanic men in the program as well. Franklin Chang-Dìaz has been on eight shuttle missions, and Michael Lopez-Alegria has walked in space."

"Are you excited about going into space, Ms. Washington?" Jessica asked.

"Absolutely. This is what I have prepared for all my life," she replied with feeling.

"Do you believe in life on other planets, Ms. Washington?" Ziggy asked politely.

"I believe in possibilities," she told him as she touched him on the shoulder. "That's why I'm in this program."

The group walked slowly back to Rocket Park, each one thinking of hope and dreams.

8

"SHE WAS REALLY COOL, MON," ZIGGY SAID TO Jerome as he skipped down the path.

"I can't believe we met a real live astronaut!" Rashawn said with excitement.

"Do you think if I showed her this thing I found that she could tell us what it is, mon?" Ziggy took the strange object out of his pocket. It seemed to catch the sunlight, and it almost seemed to glow in his hand.

"Don't bother her with silly stuff like that, Ziggy," Rico replied. "She's much too important to deal with your imaginary space stuff."

"I guess you're right, mon." Ziggy sighed and put it back in his pocket.

As they got closer to Rocket Park, Samantha turned to the group and asked, "Are you guys ready for the Space Shot and the G-Force Accelerator?"

"Ooh, ready, mon!" Ziggy said eagerly as they hurried over to the area where the outside simulators stood waiting.

Ms. Washington still walked with them. "I think I'll stick around and watch. You're the best team at Space Camp!"

"You got that right, ma'am!" Rico said proudly.

"Our first simulation is the Space Shot," Samantha said. "Since we've been talking with Astronaut Washington about really going into space, this is the perfect time to experience it."

"Why don't you ride with us?" Jerome suggested to Ms. Washington. "Since you haven't really been in space, maybe you can use this for practice."

"Oh, I've had plenty of practice—in simulators that make this one look like a Pogo Stick, but sure, I'll experience it with you."

They walked over to the Space Shot, which had padded seats surrounding a very tall pole. Each team member, and Ms. Washington as well, climbed into a seat, got strapped in, and prepared to be shot 140 feet straight up into the air in an instant.

"You'll feel four g's of force as you go up, you'll be weightless for about two seconds, and then you'll rush back to the ground in what feels like a free fall," she explained to Ziggy, who was strapped to the seat next to her. "Are you ready?"

Ziggy nodded, but he looked worried. Suddenly, *WHOOSH!* The seats were launched into the air, and Ziggy didn't even have time to scream. His hair went straight up as his body rushed straight down. By the time they landed, he had found his voice. "Zowie! I have found my destiny! Let's do it again!"

Samantha, watching from the ground and holding everyone's glasses and flip-flops, let them ride a second time. This time, Ziggy managed to scream before the air was forced from his lungs.

"Whee! You are really lucky, Ms. Washington," he

said to her as they were being unstrapped, "to get to do cool stuff like this every day."

"Not all of it is rides in simulators like this. We have to do math and science calculations and lots of reading as well," she explained as they were unlatched from the seat and headed back to the cafeteria.

"Did they teach you about the monkeynauts in space school?" Neil asked. His red spiked hair seemed to stand up even higher after the Space Shot simulator ride.

Alan, whose hair matched his brother's wind-tossed spikes, added, "Ziggy thinks the monkeys were really space creatures in disguise." He laughed a little and tried to make his voice sound like he doubted Ziggy, but he looked directly at the astronaut as he spoke.

"I don't think Abel and Baker were Martians, if that's what you're asking," she replied with sincerity. "They were just little monkeys who helped us figure out how to live outside the boundaries of this earth."

"So who takes the bananas?" Rico asked. "Ziggy thinks that aliens are to blame."

"Hey, mon! Everybody keeps saying what Ziggy thinks, mon, and making me sound like I'm wacked!" He looked around and grinned. "Well, maybe I am, but suppose I'm right? Suppose the bananas really *are* being eaten by the space creatures that live in the giant shuttle in Rocket Park. What if what we think are just skinny brown squirrels are really spacemen checking us out? Suppose nothing is as it seems and I'm right?"

No one answered for a moment.

Finally Ms. Washington took a deep breath and spoke. "Let's all sit down for a moment—right here on the grass. Is that okay, Samantha?"

Samantha nodded, looking as interested as the kids.

Ms. Washington began, "You are a dreamer, Ziggy, and that's probably the best thing in the world you can be. All young people should have imaginations like yours. It's always been dreamers who change the world by making new and wonderful discoveries."

Cubby raised his hand, as if he were in school. "You

mean like Christopher Columbus and Galileo?"

"Yes. Exactly. Columbus didn't think the world was flat, as many people of his time assumed it was. Folks then believed if a ship went too far, it would fall off the edge of the earth!"

"That's silly," Jessica said, laughing. "Everybody knows the world is round."

"But hundreds of years ago, everybody didn't. Columbus was a dreamer who looked at things differently. And in Galileo's time, people thought the earth, not the sun, was the center of our universe," Ms. Washington explained.

"The Wright brothers believed that airplanes could work," Nicolina added.

"Good! So, what I'm trying to say is that even though the bananas are probably taken away each night by the sanitation crew, and the *Pathfinder* shuttle is filled with cement . . ." She glanced up at a brown squirrel scampering in an oak tree near them. "And even though that's probably really a squirrel, that doesn't mean that Ziggy is wrong to wonder or to question or to push the limits of his imagination."

"See, I told you!" Ziggy said.

Samantha nodded. "Ziggy may very well be an explorer or discoverer of things we've never dreamed of," she added.

"If it's strange food combinations, I think he's already there!" Rashawn said, smiling. "At lunch today he put green Jell-O in his taco!"

"Ooh, yuck!" they all said as they got up and headed down the path once more.

As they headed toward the Habitat, Ziggy touched the pocket of his pants. He took a deep breath and seemed to make a decision. "Hey, Ms. Washington. Thanks for making me look not so dumb out there. My mind just grabs on to ideas and rides with them, you know."

She laughed and looked at him kindly. "That's the mind of a future astronaut for sure!"

"May I ask you one more thing?"

"Sure, Ziggy, go ahead. I love the way your group is so observant and asks so many good questions."

Ziggy removed the strange, shiny item from his pocket. "I hope you don't think this is dumb." He held it in his fist. "Can you look at this for me? My friends think this is just another example of my imagination working overtime because I was sure it came from space or something."

Ms. Washington gasped and reached out her hand for Ziggy's green stone. He handed it to her, and she grasped it gently. "Where did you find this, Ziggy?"

"On the floor near the moon gravity simulator. Is it . . . uh . . . from space?"

"No, it isn't." She took a deep breath. "It came from Chicago."

"Huh?" Ziggy looked confused. "How do you know?"

"Because it belongs to me. My grandmother gave it to me when I was a little girl. It's very old—an antique. I think her grandmother had given it to her, so it is extremely special to me. You have no idea how important this is to me."

Ziggy looked at it again. "Really? What is it?"

"It's a brooch—you know—a decorative pin, at least part of it. We had a formal NASA event here last night—that's why I'm here in Huntsville—and I wore my grandmother's pin on my dress because it was pretty, and unusual, and it matched my outfit. I didn't discover until I got back to the hotel that the stone had fallen out. I was really upset when I thought I'd lost it."

"I'm glad I found it for you," Ziggy said, "but

I really wanted it to be from another planet." He sounded disappointed.

Ms. Washington looked at him with a twinkle in her eye. "Of course, I have no idea of what really happened, but the story in our family is that my great-great grandmother discovered the stone in a cornfield, and that when she picked it up, it was glowing."

"Wow! So it's *possible* that it came from Mars?" Ziggy said. "Isn't it possible that early Martian explorers came here a long time ago and left it by mistake?"

"I'm going to let you believe that, Ziggy, because dreams are what will get you into space. If you're right, then you'll have something to talk about when Captain Ziggy is the first human to make contact with beings from another world."

"I know you're just saying that to make a kid not feel stupid, but I'm not going to forget, mon. When I am an astronaut, I will be sure to ask them about the stone they left behind!" Ziggy replied with a grin.

THE NEXT MORNING, AFTER CLEANING UP THE Habitat, packing their dirty clothes, and marching down to breakfast for the last time, the team got ready for their graduation from Space Camp.

"It's been quite a ride," Neil said.

Alan, who always seemed to speak after his brother, nodded in agreement. "It was really cool getting to know you guys," he said to Ziggy, Rashawn, Rico, and Jerome.

"Yeah, man. Same here," Rashawn added with feeling.

"What did you say the name of your club was?" Cubby asked.

"The Black Dinosaurs club," Jerome replied. "We have a clubhouse back home and passwords and everything."

"Cool!" Cubby said.

"You got girls in your club?" Jessica asked.

"Not yet. You want to be the first female member?" Rico asked her with a grin.

"No way!" she told him. "But we might start our own club when we get home."

"What kind of stuff does your club do?" Amy asked. "Good deeds and stuff?"

Rico scratched his head. "I don't think we ever came across a good deed we could do."

"We'd do good deeds if we could find any, mon!" Ziggy added. "But we don't live in a book. Our neighborhood is probably a lot like yours—pretty boring."

"We *did* once dig for treasure, though," Rashawn reminded his friends.

"But we found a box of bones, not gold," Rico said.

"Most kids who dig for treasure only find dirt!" Jessica said. "You're lucky."

"We also got trapped in a tunnel under our school once, and then we got lost in the woods on a campout," Jerome told the others. "Both times we got rescued just in time, and once we got our picture in the newspaper!"

"Awesome," Nicolina said quietly.

"The Black Dinosaurs is a really cool club, mon!" Ziggy said with pride. "Sometimes we solve mysteries and sometimes we just eat pizza in our clubhouse. Either way, we have fun!"

"This trip to Space Camp was sort of a Black Dinosaurs adventure too. Rico's dad drove us here," Rashawn explained.

Just as he said that, Rico's father, looking rested and relaxed, joined them at the table in the cafeteria. "Hey, Dad!" Rico cried out with pleasure. "Want to meet Team America?"

Rico introduced Samantha, then Cubby, Neil, and

Alan, as well as the girls. "We had a great time, Dad! We tested the simulators, went on a mission, and learned more stuff than I ever wanted to know about space!"

His father laughed.

"And we learned how astronauts go to the bathroom, mon!" Ziggy shouted loud enough for the whole cafeteria to hear. Everyone seemed to stop talking as they looked over to where they were sitting. Ziggy continued, a little quieter, "And we got to meet an astronaut!"

"Really? Who?"

"Denise Washington!" Rico replied excitedly. "She's cool!"

Rico's dad smiled. "I'm really impressed. All of you look a couple of months older, not a couple of days. You really seemed to have matured a little."

"Even Ziggy?" Rico teased.

"Especially Ziggy!"

Ziggy shook his head, flinging his braids, and took his tray back to the disposal area. There, tossing her breakfast trash into the wastebasket, stood

Astronaut Washington. She wore the light blue one-piece jumpsuit that the astronauts wore in the pictures he saw on television. He gulped. "Good morning," Ziggy said, quieter than usual.

"Good morning, Ziggy," she replied pleasantly. "Are you ready for graduation?"

"Yes, ma'am," he replied. "But I kinda hate to go home."

"I understand exactly how you feel," she told him. "But you can always come back, you know."

"I'm glad I got to meet a real astronaut," Ziggy said. "And I'm glad she was a smart, pretty black lady," he admitted shyly.

She laughed heartily. "That's the nicest thing anyone has ever said to me, Ziggy! I'll never forget you, that's for sure."

"Will you think about me when you go up in space?" He hopped from one foot to the other, a little nervous.

"As a matter of fact, I fixed my grandmother's brooch last night, and it is one of the few personal things I intend to take with me. Without you, it might have been lost forever. So, absolutely, I will think of you when I launch into space!"

"Cool, mon!" Ziggy said with a grin.

"I have to hurry now," she told him. "I have some official duties to attend to." She left the cafeteria, and Ziggy headed back to Team America.

"Is everyone ready to head over to graduation?" Samantha asked. "Where's Ziggy?" She counted the group and frowned.

"Here I am, mon!" Ziggy cried. "I was talking to Astronaut Washington."

"Where?" Cubby asked. "I don't see her."

"I wanted to introduce her to you, Dad," Rico said.

"She said she had something official to do, mon," Ziggy told them.

Samantha looked disappointed. "Sorry you missed her, Mr. Roman. I think Team America learned quite a bit from her." She gathered up her bag and clipboard and told the group, "Let's go, Team America. Time for graduation."

The team marched over to the auditorium and

waited in line with the other teams that had been at Space Camp that week: Team Enterprise, Team Discovery, and many others. Finally, when their name was called, Team America marched in proudly, heads held high, large smiles of accomplishment on their faces. Each name was called and each member of the team received flight "wings" and a certificate of graduation. Parents snapped pictures from the back of the room.

After the welcomes and the speeches and lots of applause, the camp director said, "I have a special guest to introduce to you. Please welcome Astronaut Denise Washington!"

Everyone in the auditorium cheered and applauded, especially Team America.

Rico turned and saw his father, who was sitting in the back with the rest of the parents. "I told you!" he mouthed.

His father nodded and grinned.

Ms. Washington walked to the speakers' stand and smiled at the group. "Space. The final frontier. I sound like the start of an old TV show, don't I?

But there is so much out there to explore and discover that it will take a thousand lifetimes to learn it all. Our knowledge of space is so vast right now, compared to what the cavemen knew, for example. But what we still have to learn makes us feel like specks in a bottomless ocean. I want all of you to be thirsty for knowledge, eager to question, and willing to explore all possibilities. Now that you are Space Camp graduates, all of you have that potential."

Everyone applauded. She paused and looked at her notes. "I had the opportunity to meet one of the teams who just graduated—Team America," she continued.

Ziggy and his friends exchanged self-conscious smiles.

"Although we focus on the team here rather than the individual, there is one young man I would like to thank personally."

Ziggy felt a little nervous excitement starting to grow in his stomach.

"This young man, who embodies the spirit of curiosity, sometimes to the extreme"—she smiled and looked into the audience—"this young man found a piece of jewelry that I had lost. It had great personal importance to me, and I want to thank him personally. Ziggy Colwin, will you come to the stage, please?"

Team America exploded in cheers of joy as Ziggy made his way to the front, grinning from ear to ear.

As he climbed on to the stage, Ms. Washington continued. "Of course, Ziggy thought it was an artifact from outer space—actually, he thought lots of things here were the work of space aliens—but that's the spirit we try to encourage here."

Everyone laughed a little.

"Ziggy," she said as he stood next to her. His braids seemed to be in motion as he looked around, shaking a little. "I wish to give you this special award."

From the podium she took a medallion that hung on a red-, white-, and blue-striped ribbon and placed it around his neck. Ziggy, suddenly shy, whispered his thanks.

"Ladies and gentlemen, please recognize Ziggy Colwin, future astronaut and space explorer, who now wears the title of 'Captain of Creativity'!"

Ziggy bowed three or four times, spun around twice, then bowed again. The audience roared and laughed and clapped. Team America hooted and cheered until Ms. Washington said, "Okay, Ziggy, you can sit down now!"

Ziggy, all grins and nervous energy, thanked her once more and bounded from the stage. "Don't ever doubt the captain, mon!" he whispered to his friends as he sat back down. They gave him high fives, and everyone had to look at the medallion and exclaim over it.

Finally all the teams were dismissed, and Space Camp was officially over. Ziggy and the rest of the Black Dinosaurs shook hands with Alan and Neil and Cubby, as well as the three girls. They promised to keep in touch by e-mail, but they all knew they probably wouldn't. Everyone gave Samantha a final hug as parents gathered up their kids and headed to the cars to return to the real world.

"I'll never forget Team America," she told them with feeling. They waved and headed to the parking lot.

"So, was it worth it?" Rico's father asked as he started up the car.

"Couldn't have been better, mon!" Ziggy said, sighing contentedly as he snuggled into his pillow in the corner of the backseat. He touched the medallion around his neck and smiled to himself.

"Wait till we get back to school and tell the rest of the kids about this!" Rico said.

"This was better than getting to level ninety-nine on the Mega Mighty Martian Blasters video game, mon!" Ziggy said.

"Did you find any space creatures like you talked about before you left?" Rico's dad asked.

The four friends looked at each other and grinned. "Well, Ziggy found some suspicious-looking bananas," Rashawn began. He was trying to hold back a laugh.

"And he discovered some squirrels that might have been from Mars—we didn't look real close," Jerome added, almost bursting into laughter.

"And we found a space vehicle that *maybe* some space creatures might have used to hide in," Rico continued, giggling. "But they'd have to eat cement, because that's what it was filled with!"

The four friends laughed together as they told Mr. Roman about their adventures. "Actually, Ziggy did find out that Ms. Washington's stone was over two hundred years old," Rashawn said. "Maybe it really could have been left here by visitors from another planet."

"Maybe as a club we can check out some stuff about space invaders on the Internet or at the library when we get home," Jerome suggested.

"I guess there's no way to really know for sure," Rico said sensibly.

"I know because I believe, mon. I still believe there's something or someone out there," Ziggy said as he gazed out the window toward the afternoon sky. "One day I'll find out. You'll see."

The four friends dozed as the car headed north, speeding back toward Cincinnati, where more adventures awaited the Black Dinosaurs.

HERE'S A SNEAK PEEK INTO
THE NEXT CLUBHOUSE MYSTERY,

THE BACKYARD ANIMAL SHOW

"THEY REALLY DO LOOK LIKE BEASTS, DON'T THEY, mon?" Ziggy said in quiet appreciation of the snorting machines across the street.

The huge yellow backhoe looked almost graceful as it scooped dirt from an increasingly large hole. Its long neck dipped, scraped, and pulled huge clods of earth, pebbles and branches dangling from its claw teeth like the remains of a meal. It turned, swiveled, and spit the rocky clumps into the back of the dump trucks, which then ambled away like overburdened elephants.

"The man inside the cabin who's operating the

controls looks like one of those toy men we used to play with," Rashawn observed.

"Look at the treads on those rollers, man," Jerome said. "I bet that thing can roll over and stomp a whole army of toy builders."

"You think they run on diesel fuel?" Rico asked.

"For sure, mon," Ziggy replied. "Big rigs need heavy-duty food—just like I do. For dinner my mum is making sirloin steak covered with bananas! Yummy."

"Yuck," said Rashawn, who did not eat meat. "Just give me a big bowl of chili instead."

"Whoa! Look at that! The crane is lifting that tree like it's a toothpick!" Jerome pointed out with excitement.

"Where will they take the tree?" Rico asked.

"I don't know, mon," Ziggy answered. "Maybe they'll make a chair out of it. Or a house for some-one to live in. Or maybe just a pile of wooden tooth-picks." He sighed.

"The trees were home to lots of creatures," Rico continued glumly. "The birds and the snakes and the raccoons and the deer that lived in those bushes and woods were happy living there. Now it's all just dirt so people can build apartments. It doesn't seem fair to me."

"The animals will find another place to live, Rico," Jerome said, trying to sound reassuring.

"Where?" Rico asked. "My mother told me they're building another new housing project a few blocks away. Pretty soon there won't be any place left for the creatures."

The boys turned their attention to the street in front of them as they heard the harsh screeching of truck brakes, followed by a soft thud. The dirty yellow dump truck, full of rocks and debris from the work zone, had been rumbling slowly down the street when it stopped suddenly. The boys watched as the driver jumped out of the cab and ran to the side of the road.

"Oh, no!" cried Rico. "The truck hit a deer!"